For my mom and dad, who taught me plant Latin and patience,
and how to love our precious green world

— KIRSTEN

To my best friend, Carrie, and our friendship and growth

— CARMEN

SLEEPING BEAR PRESS™

10 9 8 7 6 5 4 3 2 1

Library of Congress Cataloging-in-Publication Data
Names: Pendreigh, Kirsten, author. | Mok, Carmen, illustrator.
Title: Luna's green pet / Kirsten Pendreigh ; [illustrated by] Carmen Mok.
Description: Ann Arbor, MI : Sleeping Bear Press, [2022] | Audience: Ages
4-8. | Audience: Grades 2-3. | Summary: A young girl named Luna
circumvents her apartment building's no-pet policy by rescuing a
houseplant which she names Stephanie.
Identifiers: LCCN 2022003568 | ISBN 9781534111615 (hardcover)
Subjects: CYAC: House plants—Fiction. | Pets—Fiction. | LCGFT: Picture books.
Classification: LCC PZ7.1.P4457 Lu 2022 | DDC [E]—dc23
LC record available at https://lccn.loc.gov/2022003568

LUNA'S
Green Pet

By Kirsten Pendreigh and illustrated by Carmen Mok

PUBLISHED by SLEEPING BEAR PRESS™

Luna longed for a pet, but her apartment building had a very *strict* NO PETS! policy.

No **dogs**, no cats, no rodents, no reptiles, no birds.

Not even GOLDFISH, after
Mr. Cousteau's aquarium spill.

Luna's friends had lots of advice.

"What about a pet rock?"

No.

"Or a pet-a-guchi!"

Nope.

"An ant farm?"

Uh, no.

Luna was ready to give up.

And then . . . she saw it.

"You're lucky I came along," said Luna.
"You need a lot of love."

Luna's new pet had a long
and complicated name.

"I'll just call you Stephanie,"
said Luna.

Luna gave Stephanie
a bigger crate,

new bedding,

and fresh water.

Stephanie perked up.

Each night, Luna read
Stephanie a story.

Each morning, she walked her to the park,
which Stephanie *mostly* enjoyed.

Luna's friends were not impressed with her green pet.

"Does she make any sounds?"

"Can she do any tricks?"

Luna rolled her eyes.

To her, Stephanie was perfect,

if a little rambunctious.

Luna gave Stephanie a trim,

a collar,

and obedience training.

Then . . . strange clumps of bumps appeared.

"Oh, Stephanie! Is that a rash?

A sunburn?

A moonburn?!"

The bumps grew.

Luna tried bandages,

sponge baths,

and hugs.

But the bumps got bigger.

"I'm taking you to the botanist first thing in the morning!"

During the night . . .
by the light of the moon . . .

the bumps burst open!

A powerful perfume woke Luna.
"Stephanie! Is that you? Am I dreaming?"
Luna wasn't dreaming.

Soon, exotic visitors began to arrive!

By day . . .

and by night!

Luna decided to enter Stephanie in the pet parade,
where she won a special prize.

BEST IN SCENT

Now Luna's friends wished they had a Stephanie too!

And Stephanie had another trick up her sleeve.

"Is she pregnant?"

"Is that an avocado?"

"Can we make guacamole?"

When the pod burst apart,
a tangle of tufted seeds lay inside.

Luna saved one seed for each friend,
and one for each neighbor.

The rest she floated away on the warm light wind.

"Someone out there is waiting to love their own Stephanie,"
Luna said. "I just know it."

Why Houseplants Make Great Pets

- Plants are quiet. They never bark at the mail carrier!
- Plants are good listeners.
- Plants don't need walks every day. They don't even have to go out to pee!
- Plants help you do your homework:
  Studies show students in classrooms with plants do better on tests and assignments than students in classrooms with no plants.
- Plants help clean your house:
  Their leaves absorb airborne toxins.
  They release oxygen and moisture to help you breathe more easily.
- Plants reduce stress:
  Taking care of plants makes people feel calmer and happier.
- Plants give you gifts:
  Plants like Stephanie produce beautiful, fragrant flowers.
  Aloe vera has sap to soothe sunburns or help heal a cut.
  Lemon trees give you fruit.

Ten Easy Plants for Your First Green Pet

- Spider plants (*Chlorophytum comosum*): Purify the air and grow little babies!
- Snake plants (*Dracaena trifasciata*): Don't worry, they don't bite!
- Christmas cactus (*Schlumbergera*): Merry pink flowers even when it's not Christmas!
- African violets (*Saintpaulia*): Pretty purple and pink flowers with fuzzy leaves to stroke.
- Lucky bamboo (*Dracaena sanderiana*): Grows in water and can be trained into cool shapes!
- Air plants (*Tillandsia*): Grow without soil or water!
- Ponytail palm (*Beaucarnea recurvata*): Who doesn't want a giant ponytail in their room?
- Dragon tree (*Dracaena marginata*): Fortunately, dragon trees don't breathe fire!
- Polka dot plants (*Hypoestes phyllostachya*): Leaves covered in fun spots!
- Succulents! Many types! All love sunlight.

Feeling more adventurous?

- Try an insect-eating plant like the tropical sundew (*Drosera*).
  Just remember, these carnivorous plants are trickier to take care of (and you might have to hunt for insects to feed them!).

More about Stephanie
(Stephanotis Floribunda)

Stephanotis floribunda has three names. *Stephanotis floribunda* is its official scientific name. It combines the Greek word for "crown" (*stephanos*) with the Greek word for "ear" (*otis*) because the flowers are arranged like a crown and each petal looks like an ear. Maybe that's how Stephanie listens to her bedtime stories!

People also call *Stephanotis* "flower of the princesses" because brides often use the fragrant flowers in their bouquets. She's also called Madagascar Jasmine, since *Stephanotis* were first found on Madagascar, a warm and sunny island off the east coast of Africa. There, *Stephanotis floribunda* have beautiful pollinator friends: bees, butterflies, and hummingbirds visit in the daytime, and hawk moths flutter in at night.

The hawk moths are attracted to *Stephanotis*'s perfume, which is much stronger at night. *Stephanotis* releases its fragrance in waves at special times—early in the evening and just before the sun rises. Hungry hawk moths—some as big as hot dogs!—unfurl their long proboscises to reach down into the *Stephanotis* flower for nectar. *Stephanotis* also has lovely glossy green leaves, which animals like Australian possums like to munch on.

Owning Your Own *Stephanotis*

If you live in a warm place, you could grow *Stephanotis* outside. Just watch out for hungry possums! Inside, *Stephanotis* likes a warm, bright room, with its roots in good potting soil and just the right amount of watering.

In the wild, *Stephanotis* gets its "food" naturally, when leaves around it decay and feed the soil. In a pot, it will need you to fertilize it every few months. And every two years it will need a bigger pot, or its growing roots will break right through. Kind of like what your toes might do if you stayed in your baby shoes too long!

Once *Stephanotis* flowers fade and wilt, you can remove them and give your plant a little haircut. This might encourage it to flower again. If it grows a big seedpod, about the size of a small avocado, you can wait for it to burst open. Then, like Luna, you can share the feathery seeds with your friends!

And, when you're older, if you want to work with plants, you could study to become a botanist (a scientist who studies plants), a horticulturalist (a scientist who grows plants), or a florist!

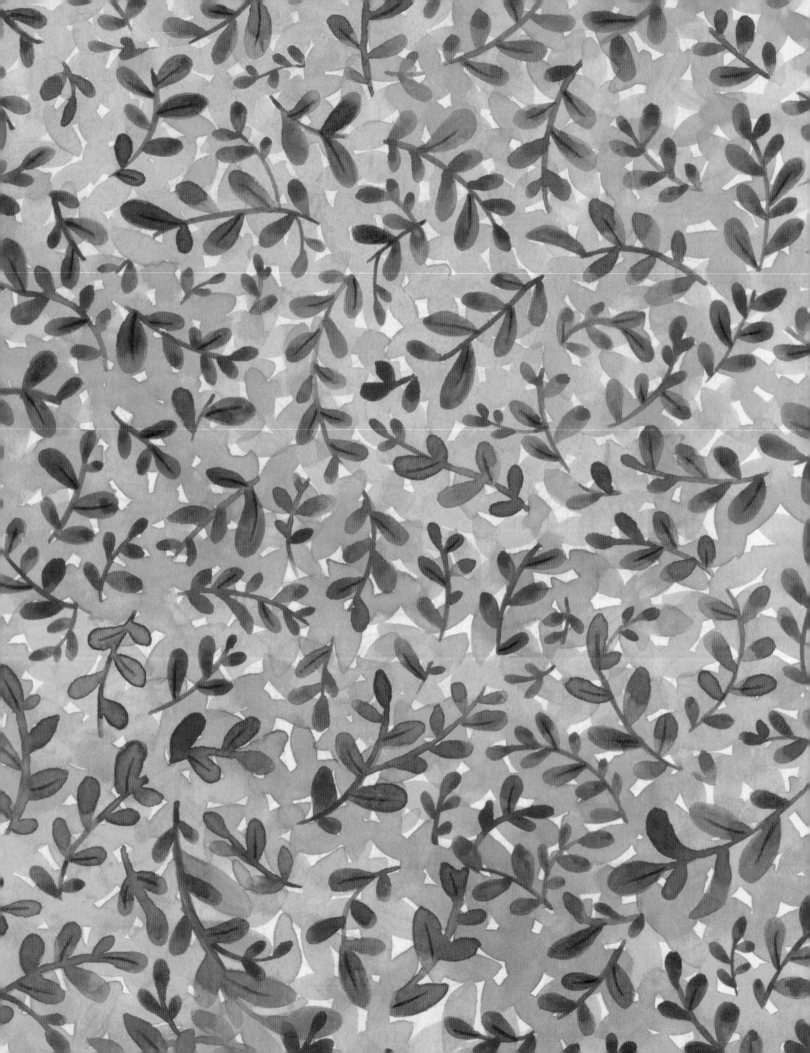